Terror 9/11

a novel

by

DOUG PATON

H·I·P Books

HIP Sr. novels

National Library of Canada Cataloguing in Publication Data

Paton, Doug, 1980–
    Terror 911 / Doug Paton.

(New Series Canada)
ISBN 0-9731237-6-1

I. Title. II. Series.
PS8581.A78396T47 2003   jC813'.6   C2003-901677-3
PR9199.3.P3436T47 2003

General editor: Paul Kropp
Text Design: Laura Brady
Illustrations drawn by: Matt Melanson
Cover design: Robert Corrigan

2 3 4 5 6 7   07 06

Printed and bound in Canada by Webcom

High Interest Publishing is an imprint of the Chestnut Publishing group. We acknowledge the support of the Government of Canada through the Book Publishing Industry Development Program (BPIDP) for our publishing activities.

Curtis was just picking up his sister at the World Trade Center when the first plane hit. As the north tower bursts into flames, the teenager must fight to save his sister, his dad and himself.

CHAPTER 1

I Didn't Want to Go

I didn't want to go into the city that morning. The new school year had just begun and I had promised to do better. No more disasters, I told myself. Not like last year—flunking both math and science. This new year was going to go better, and that meant a better start. It meant not missing any classes.

But someone had to pick up my kid sister, Allie. My mom couldn't afford to take time off work to get her. My dad was always "too busy" to bring Allie all the way to our house in New Jersey, or so he said. That left just me.

"Mom, I really don't want to do this," I said. "I promised that I was going to do better in school this year. That means I actually have to, like, *go* to class."

"I know, honey, but I really need you to pick up Allie from your father's office," she said. "I have a big meeting at work today, and your sister can't take the train out here all by herself. She's only seven, you know."

"How come Dad can't take the time off work to bring her home? Why does he always make us do it?" I asked. "What makes him so important?"

"Your father's a stubborn man, Curtis," my mom replied. She was spraying some gunk on her hair, not really looking at me. "He always has been like that and he's not going to change anytime soon. You and your father have some things in common, you know."

What she meant is that we're both stubborn. Dad is stubborn about all sorts of things, mostly

about putting in 12 hours a day at work. He's made it big in the business world. Now he's got an office way up in the World Trade Center. If you asked him, he'd say that being stubborn is what got him into one of the tallest buildings in the world.

But I'm not stubborn like Dad. It's not like I've

got some sort of goal that's stuck in my mind. It's not like I can't change what I do or how I think. But it bugs me when he ends up running my life or my mom tries to do the same.

"This isn't fair," I complained. "The train ride to the city is boring. Besides, I might end up missing math class, and then I'll really be toast."

"Honey, please," Mom said. "If you leave early enough, you can make it back before your second class."

"You think so?" I asked, feeling myself giving in.

"Of course," she replied. "So long as you don't goof around coming back home, you should be fine."

"I never goof around," I snapped back. That was a lie, of course, but I was giving up the fight. Somebody had to bring my kid sister home, so I guess the somebody was me. "But you can tell Dad that he should bring Allie back himself next time. It's not my job."

Which was true. If my dad had just kept his word and brought Allie back on Sunday, there'd be no problem. But my dad was always doing a deal, even with us. So he kept my sister overnight at his place on Long Island and was bringing her to his work this morning. Then the problem was mine.

Things had been like this ever since my parents split up, back when I was nine. Allie had just been born when Dad decided that he didn't want to be part of this family anymore. He took off with some woman whose name I can't remember, and I bet he can't either. So my mom was stuck looking after both of us. I was old enough that I could help out with stuff around the house, but it still wasn't easy. Allie was a real handful and my mom's job seemed to keep her very busy. So guess who had to pick up the slack?

And we were doing just fine, really, until my dad decided that he wanted to be a part of our lives again. Allie was thrilled that her dad had come back to see her, but I didn't want to have much to do with the guy. He had left us when we needed him the most, and I couldn't forgive him.

As part of the divorce, my mom had to hand Allie over to my dad for two weekends a month. The "visit" was from Friday night to Sunday night.

My dad always managed to bring my sister back late or the next day. He mostly had lousy excuses. "The car broke down on the Long Island Expressway." "The trains are all running late." "Allie's so tired, she'd be better off sleeping here."

That's what got to me. He expected some poor slave—me—to go pick the kid up. *Great*, I thought, as I tucked my math book under my arm.

The train ride to New York was boring. I never liked taking the train, but it was often the fastest way to get into the city. At seven in the morning, the train was packed. There wasn't even room to open my math book and study.

The train line ran past a lot of old warehouses and some stinking chemical plants. This was New Jersey. On the other side of the Hudson was Manhattan. My dad's office was in the World Trade Center, the famous twin towers. These were the tallest buildings in New York—110 storeys packed with people. Up at the top was a restaurant called Windows on the World. My dad took Allie and me up there once. The view was great, but the food was a bit fancy for me. I guess it's all what you like.

My train headed under the Hudson River. This was the part of the trip that I hated the most. For five minutes the train crawled through a dark tunnel, tons of water over our heads. I'd been down here once when the train stopped dead. For 20 minutes we sat, wondering what had gone wrong.

When you're stuck under a river, you end up thinking about all that water over your head. You start thinking the air is getting thick. You start smelling smoke when there isn't any. You start to wonder if you'll ever get out.

A rotten way to die, I told myself. If my number is up, I want to go kicking and screaming—not trapped and fighting to breathe.

CHAPTER 2

Picking up Allie

I got off the subway one stop early. The IRT line was jammed that morning—bodies pushed into bodies. I had to get out just to get some air.

Up in front of me loomed the World Trade Center towers, the biggest in New York. It figures that my dad would work there. New York's biggest ego in New York's biggest building.

I had to admit that the twin towers looked pretty nice. The sky was clear and the morning sun

made the buildings shine in the distance. I read someplace that it took a million man-hours and a million tons of concrete to build them. I believe it. They were towering way above my head that morning, stretching up towards the sky.

I got to the plaza around 8:30. Dad worked up on the 60th floor of the north tower. He did some kind of big-wheel job for Mathers & Schmidt. They're a bunch of accountants who crunch numbers for Wall Street guys. I remember that Dad made me meet Mr. Mathers once, when I was little. I think I was supposed to be impressed.

Anyhow, I got on one of the elevators and began the ride up. It didn't take that long to get to Dad's floor, which was a good thing. There had to be two dozen people in that elevator, packed in like fans at a rock concert. I didn't like it much. Actually I don't like elevators even if they're empty. I don't like small, cramped spaces—or even big, cramped spaces like school. They make me feel creepy.

To make things even worse, I wasn't looking forward to seeing Dad. We hadn't got along too well ever since that girlfriend, the one whose name I don't remember. A couple years later, he tried to make it up to me, but I've stayed pretty cool.

So I stopped doing the weekend visit thing. I even stopped talking to him on the phone. He kept saying that Mom was "making him look like the bad guy." But it wasn't Mom who did it; it was Dad himself.

When I asked for Dad at the front desk, the woman pointed to a small office down the hall. I got closer, took a deep breath and calmed myself down. No, I didn't want to be here, I didn't want to be the Allie-transport guy, but I wasn't going to make a big deal about it. *Get the kid and get out,* I said to myself.

Dad was sitting with his back to me when I came in. He was looking at a computer screen filled with numbers. *What a job,* I thought. When my dad was young, he used to be about my size, but now he must be close to 300 pounds. That's what a desk job does to you.

"Dad," I said to get his attention.

He turned in his chair and smiled. "Curtis! I'm glad you showed up."

The old man seemed almost happy to see me. I guess he just wanted to dump Allie and get on with his work.

"Where's Allie?" I asked him. "I'm in a bit of a hurry."

"She's checking out the copy machine, I think, just down the hall," he said. "Are you sure you can't stay for a bit and talk? We haven't had a chance to see each other lately."

"I have to get back to school before my second

14

class starts." My voice sounded as cold as I felt in my heart.

Dad gave me a funny look. "Since when have you cared so much about school?" he asked me.

I was about to say something when Allie came bouncing into the office. She was holding a sheet of paper in her hands, waving it around.

"Daddy, look! I copied my hand!" she declared. You'd think the copy machine was the greatest thing in the world.

It took Allie a while to notice me. "Awwh," she groaned. "I guess it's time to leave."

"It sure is, kid," I told her. "I have to get you to school before I miss any more classes. Now get your backpack and we're out of here."

"I'm ready," she said. "I just want to put my hand picture in my backpack so I can show the kids at school. Isn't it cool, Curtis?"

"Yeah, coolest Xerox of a hand that I ever saw. You sure you got everything?" I asked her. Allie was famous for leaving things behind. If the girl's head wasn't attached, she'd leave that behind, too.

"Got it all," she replied. "I've got my toothbrush, my jammies and my book. And now I've got Bear," she said, reaching to grab this stinky old stuffed bear she liked to cuddle. "I'm all set."

She went over to Dad to kiss him goodbye. "Bye, Daddy! I'll see you next time," she said. "Just 12 sleeps, right?"

"Right," he said. "You keep out of trouble and try not to drive your mother crazy, all right?" he replied.

"I promise," she said, crossing her heart to make it a pledge.

"And, Allie," Dad added, "don't forget your puffer." He picked up the blue puffer that Allie used for her asthma. My sister just giggled.

Dad looked at me as I turned to leave. "Hey, don't be a stranger, Curtis. You're welcome to come over anytime you want. There's lots of room at my new apartment."

I didn't say anything in return. I'd never seen the place where he lived—hadn't seen the last one either. I couldn't see any point in going from New Jersey to Long Island just to see a piece of real estate. Besides, my friends were at home, not at his place.

I ignored him. "C'mon, Allie, we gotta go."

Allie and I walked to the elevator in silence. Mostly she talks your ear off, but today Allie must have been tired. She didn't say a word.

When we got to the elevator, I pushed the button and waited. I was getting antsy about the time. I looked at my watch to figure out if I could get to school in time. It was September 11, 8:46 a.m.

The explosion was at exactly 8:46.

CHAPTER 3

The Building Shook

Allie and I froze. Neither of us knew what had just happened. The sound was a dull boom. It was like the noise you get during construction, a mix of a boom and a thud.

But this was big—huge. I could feel the building start to shake, as if it had been hit by a giant hammer. I could sense the movement with my feet, and then it looked as if the walls were moving.

For a second, it felt as if we were all in slow

motion. The building leaned one way, then back the other. I braced myself with my feet. When the motion stopped, the whole building felt like it was sinking.

"Curtis, what was that?" Allie asked me.

"Wish I knew," I told her. "Maybe we should go ask Dad what's going on."

I turned and saw that the woman at the front desk was on her phone. Her face was white, and she was trying to phone somebody downstairs. A few other people came out of their offices and began looking around, wondering what had happened. There didn't seem to be much wrong, but the sound and motion had been scary.

As other people began coming out of their offices, we walked to Dad's. Nobody seemed to be worried. I'd say that people were curious, kind of wondering what had happened. There sure weren't any alarm bells or sirens. There was nothing to let us know that we were in big trouble.

Our dad was looking out the window when we came running back to his office. Whatever had just happened didn't seem to bother him at all.

"You forget something?" he asked.

"No, we came back to make sure everything is all right. Did you hear the noise?"

"Yeah, I heard it," Dad replied. He tilted back in his chair and put his hands behind his head. "Must be construction out there. Every time you turn around somebody is putting up a new building."

"Yeah, but it sounded so big," I said. "The whole building seemed to move."

"Well, I wouldn't worry about it. They built these towers to handle earthquakes. A couple of years ago, some guys even blew up the parking garage and none of us felt a thing."

I remembered that. The bomb had left a big hole in the garage and killed six people, but the building barely moved.

"I felt it move, Daddy," Allie told him.

"Don't get upset, honey," Dad told her. "If something had happened, we'd have heard over the speakers."

"Yeah, well, we were just wondering," I said. I felt kind of stupid, coming back to him the way we did.

"Besides, I thought you were in a hurry to get to school. It's almost nine o'clock, you know."

Ri-ight, I felt like saying, as if I couldn't tell time myself.

Allie gave Dad another hug and we set out down the hall one more time. Allie had more to say this time. She wasn't worried about the noise anymore. Instead, Allie got telling me what she and Dad had done over the weekend. She told me about a whole day at the Bronx Zoo, of all places. Then she stopped her story right in the middle of a sentence.

"Hey, do you smell smoke?" she asked me.

"Nah," I said, "they don't let people smoke in buildings anymore."

"Not that kind of smoke," Allie said, "fire smoke."

"They don't have fires in these big buildings," I told her. "If they did, the sprinklers would come on and the alarm bells would all start ringing. It's just your imagination."

"Daddy says I have a good imagination," Allie said cheerfully.

"Yeah, right," I groaned. By now we were back out at the front, and I really did smell something. I stopped and sniffed the air. *Wait a minute*, I said to myself, *the kid is right. That's real smoke.* I began to put it all together—the sound, the motion, the smoke—and I didn't like how it was adding up.

When we got to the elevator, there was a crowd of people already there. It looked like everybody was pouring out of their offices.

"There's been an explosion!" somebody said.

"The elevator won't work," said a voice behind me. "We've got to go down the stairs!"

Down the hall, I could see out a big window. It looked like some kind of strange snowstorm was going on. All these bits of paper were floating in the air.

"What happened?" I shouted to some guy in a suit. When I looked again, I saw that it was Mr. Mathers.

"You're Patrick McIvor's kids," the guy said, smiling at us. "You two come up to visit your dad?"

I didn't answer the question. For one thing, the answer would have taken too long. For another thing, I was scared. There really was a smell of smoke ... and something else, like at an airport.

"Listen, Mr. Mathers, is this serious or what?" I asked him.

"It's probably just a fire drill," he told me. "If we don't get out in time, the fire marshal gives us a fine. So you kids had better get going down the stairs. If it's a real fire and the sprinklers go off, we could all get pretty wet in here." Mr. Mathers was smiling, as if this were a joke. But he gave me a push with one arm that made it clear where we should go.

There didn't seem to be too much choice. The elevators were all dead and people were heading to the stairs. Sixty flights down! It would be one long walk, but it was better than getting trapped in an elevator. That would really drive me nuts.

"OK, kid," I told my sister. "Looks like we're taking the stairs—you, me and Bear."

"No way," she said, shaking her head.

"Yes way," I told her. "Now let's get moving."

"But what about Daddy?" she whined. "We can't go without Daddy."

"Dad will meet us downstairs," I told her. People were streaming past us now, and some of them told us to get moving.

"We've got to go get him, Curtis," she said, making her body as stiff as a piece of stone. My sister can be very stubborn sometimes and this was one of them. It must be some kind of family trait.

"Allie," I told her, like an order.

"I'm going to cry," she threatened.

And that was enough to make me cave in. "OK, we'll go and get Dad," I grumbled. Then I grabbed Allie's hand and we headed down the hall.

I almost blew my cool when we got back to Dad's office. Our old man wasn't there—and neither was his briefcase.

"Look, he's taken off already," I said.

"I bet he's gone to find us," she said. "We should try and find him first."

She had so much faith in Dad that sometimes it made me want to puke. Still, if he was wasting time looking for us, maybe we should return the favor. The fire would probably be out by the time we got downstairs, anyhow.

"All right, we can look for him, but we can't take too long because . . . "

"I know, I know, because you have to get to school so you don't miss any more classes," she cut in.

"No, that's not it," I said. "It's just that I think there's a fire someplace and, well . . . we've got to get out."

"But he's our dad," she said.

"OK, but if we don't find him in two minutes, we take the stairs and leave. Two minutes, at the very most," I repeated.

The smoke was getting thicker. And now I recognized the other smell—the airport smell. It was jet fuel.

CHAPTER 4

Where's Dad? Where's Allie?

The first place we looked for Dad was at the elevators. There was nobody in sight. By now, the offices and halls were almost empty. Then we checked near the stairs, hoping that he might have waited for us there.

Nobody.

The smell of smoke and jet fuel was starting to get stronger, and I was really worried. It was getting harder to see and breathe, even for me. Allie was coughing a lot.

"Use your puffer," I told her, "then we have to go."

Allie took two quick puffs, then coughed a little. She seemed to feel better, so I grabbed her hand and got ready to leave. We were right at the stairs when I heard more coughing from nearby.

"That's Daddy," Allie shouted.

I knew she was right. My dad has had smoker's hack most of his life, and that sounded just like his cough. The sound came from just down the hall, and that's where we found him.

"Daddy!" Allie screamed in delight.

"Oh, sweetie," he said, as he hugged her tightly. "I've been looking all over for you two. We need to get out of here fast. Something really terrible has happened."

I looked at my father to see if he'd tell me more, but he just shook his head. Something had gone wrong. But it was something he didn't want to tell me about, at least not in front of Allie.

"And Allie," he said, "you'd better leave your backpack here."

"But what if somebody steals it?" my sister asked. "It's got my hand picture!"

"I think it will be safe here in the office," my dad said, pushing one of the straps off Allie's shoulder. "The stairs are going to be pretty crowded, so there's no room for a backpack. All you really need is your puffer."

"But I'm taking Bear," Allie declared, holding her stuffed bear to her chest. "I can't leave Bear up here—he'll be scared."

Dad thought about all that for a second but decided not to make a big deal out of it. Then he took Allie's hand and we made our way back to the stairs. Both Dad and Allie were coughing, and the smoke was starting to get to me, too. We opened the door to the stairwell and found the air wasn't much better.

Even worse, the stairwell was crowded with people. They were moving pretty slowly down the stairs, but the stream was steady. There wasn't any panic. It was just a whole bunch of people going downstairs, like they might be leaving after a Yankees game.

There were lots of people coughing, but that wasn't *my* problem. My problem was that closed-in feeling. Here we were, thousands of us, crammed onto the stairs. If I thought a train tunnel was bad, this was a hundred times worse. The stairway was only two-people wide, and there were thousands of us, up and down, taking up every step. So long as we kept moving, I felt OK. But when the line stopped, when we all just stood there, that's when the creepy feeling came over me. I kept pushing it back, telling myself to stay cool and stay calm. I had to—for all of us.

Allie and I held hands so we didn't get separated; Dad was one step ahead of us. My dad was holding a handkerchief over his face. I told Allie to lift her shirt up over her nose. We had to do something to keep the smoke from getting into our lungs. As usual, Allie didn't listen. She brought her bear up to her face and covered her nose and mouth with it.

On one landing, I saw a bunch of water bottles. Somebody must have figured that we'd need them, and that somebody was right. I let go of Allie and went over to grab a couple of bottles. I figured we

31

could drink one, then use the other to wet a rag. I remembered that from some movie, putting a wet rag over your mouth to cut the smoke.

I was only gone a second, I swear, but in that second, I lost sight of them both.

"Dad?" I yelled into the crowd. "Allie?"

"Dad??" I called again, panic starting to seep into my voice.

"C'mon, guy, get moving," said a man behind me. His voice wasn't angry, but the message was clear.

"DAD!" I yelled as loud as I could.

From down below, I heard something that sounded like my name. I pushed past a few people and made my way down. When I got to the landing, Dad was waiting for me. He was looking worried and relieved at the same time.

"Thank God you're safe," he said. "But where's Allie?"

I froze. "You mean she's not with you?"

Then the nightmare really began. Allie had been holding onto my hand. She'd been trusting me to lead her out, and now . . .

"Allie!!" I screamed but got no answer.

CHAPTER 5

Going Back Up

My dad called Allie's name a couple of times, but we heard nothing. Hundreds of people were going past us now. One minute, they seemed to be going a little faster, another minute and the line stopped cold.

A short while ago, none of us had taken this seriously. It was just a fire alarm, a chance to get out of the office. Now the looks on people's faces were grim. At least some of them knew how terrible things were up above.

But our problem was here and now—Allie was missing!

"One of us has to go look for her," said Dad. "I'll go back up."

I shook my head. My dad was already having trouble breathing. He was overweight and out of shape. If he tried to go against the crowd, up the stairs, it would only make things worse for him.

"No, you stay here. I'll go," I told him, handing him a bottle of water. "It'll be easier for me to slip through the crowd because I'm smaller than you are," I said. "Besides, I'm the one who lost her."

We agreed that he'd stay on the landing and I'd go up and check the two floors above us.

"But no higher," Dad told me. "There's a big problem up there, up near the top."

"What happened?"

"A plane," he said. "A big jet smashed into the side of the building . . . and now it's on fire."

"How could that happen?" I said, not willing to believe him.

"Nobody knows," my dad told me, "but they say it wasn't an accident."

For a second I just stared at him, not willing to believe his words. This was like some kind of science fiction, a wild story that couldn't be true. A plane crashed into the Empire State Building once, years ago, but not much happened. Surely one plane couldn't do much damage to the biggest building in New York City.

But there was no time to talk, no time to think. I left my dad and pushed my way up the stairs. People kept looking at me as I tried to make my way to the landing where I got the water. At first I explained that I was looking for my kid sister, but then I stopped. The less I spoke, the less the smoke bothered me.

It kept getting worse in the stairway. The smoke got thicker, the smell got stronger, and now there was water running down the stairs. The sprinklers must have gone off on the upper floors. Now the water made the stairs slippery under my feet.

When I got up two flights of stairs, I still didn't see Allie. I tried going up another level, thinking that maybe I stopped at the wrong place. Then I started asking people if they'd seen a girl on the steps above.

"There are no kids up there," one guy told me. "Maybe somebody picked her up and is taking her downstairs." That seemed to make sense. If Allie had gotten split up from us, she'd just keep moving with the flow of people down the stairs.

Unless . . . unless she'd gotten hurt. Unless she'd gotten lost. What if we got to the bottom of the tower and Allie wasn't there? What if she got stuck in this building, trusting that her big brother would come get her?

I was on the landing for the 53rd floor, thinking hard. That's when somebody opened the fire door and came into the stairwell. In the second that the door was open, I heard a faint coughing.

"Allie?" I called into the doorway.

"Allie?" I repeated down the empty hall.

Not far away, I heard a voice I knew well. "Curtis?" she called back.

38

"Where are you, kid?" I replied. I was angry and relieved at the same time.

"I'm over here," she said.

I followed the sound of her voice to the windows. There was my sister—her teddy bear in one hand and her puffer in the other. She looked fine but really scared.

"What happened to you? Dad and I have been worried sick," I said.

"You let go of me and I kind of got in trouble," she began, holding her bear to her chest. "I couldn't find you and I couldn't find Daddy, and then this man. . . ." She seemed ready to cry.

"Yeah?"

"This man said he'd take me downstairs. But I didn't know him, and I'm not supposed to talk to strangers and . . . "

"So you came here to get away," I finished for her. I had to shake my head. All these years of streetproofing the kid, so now she runs to hide when some guy is trying to save her life.

"Come on," I said turning towards the stairs. "Dad's waiting for us downstairs."

I took her hand, firmly this time, and we started to head back down the hall. We were almost at the stairway when I took a quick look back at the window down at the end of the hall. What I saw stopped me cold.

CHAPTER 6

The Second Plane

J ust outside the big window was the south tower
of the World Trade Center. The steel and glass
tower was shining in the bright morning sun. The
sky behind the tower was clear blue. The image
could have been a postcard, it was that perfect.

But then there was this plane—a big passenger
jet—flying low. It was coming up the Hudson River,
going right towards the south tower. If the pilot
didn't pull up . . .

"What are you looking at?" Allie asked, turning around.

"Nothing," I lied.

"Come on, Curtis, we've got to—"

Her words were cut off by the explosion. I pulled Allie close to me, trying to protect her. Or maybe I was trying to stop her from seeing what I had just seen.

After the moment of impact came the sound— a dull roar that made our building shake, too. It felt like an earthquake was shaking the floor beneath us. Then I saw the flames, shooting from the entire middle of the south tower.

"Curtis, you're squooshing me," Allie whined. "What happened?"

"It was a plane, Allie," I told her. My words were flat, my voice felt numb, my heart felt as if it had stopped. "A plane just hit the other tower."

CHAPTER 7

The Real Nightmare

I tried to convince myself that this was impossible. I tried to tell myself that this was only a dream —a nightmare—and that I'd wake up in just a minute. I'd wake up and be in my bed and my mom would be telling me to go to school. I'd wake up and be worried about my math class and packing a lunch. I'd wake up to a normal life.

That's what I told myself, standing there on the

46

53rd floor, watching the flames shoot out from the south tower.

I could feel Allie pulling at my shirt and calling my name, but I couldn't respond. I kept thinking about the people on that plane, all of them dead. And the offices that it crashed into. Those people must be dead, too. It must have been like that up above us, on the upper floors of the north tower. Explosion, fire, death. How could something like this be happening?

Suddenly, my problems seemed so small. I felt ashamed that I had ever worried about missing class. Or that I hadn't wanted to pick up my sister. Or that I never went to visit my dad anymore. All that stuff seemed stupid or selfish.

Then the fear set in. I began to worry about what was going to happen next. That plane crash was no accident—that was no confused pilot. It wasn't like that lost plane that hit the Empire State Building. Now two planes had crashed into the World Trade Center, and maybe there'd be a third or a fourth one coming.

"Curtis?"

"Curtis?"

"CURTIS!"

I don't know how long I'd been standing there thinking like that. But I finally realized that Allie was calling me, and then I felt stupid. There'd be time to think later. There'd be time to think about a world that seemed to be going crazy. Right now we needed to get out of this tower, and we needed to do it fast.

I grabbed Allie's hand and headed back to the stairs. The stairway was just as crowded as it had been before, but there was more smoke now. There was so much that I could barely see. How was I going to find Dad when I couldn't even see the person in front of me? How was I going to get Allie downstairs with her coughing like she was?

We needed something to cover our faces. I pushed open the door to the 52nd floor, trying to find a piece of cloth we could use. There was nothing—just potted plants and papers. Across the way, I could see smoke pouring from the south tower.

48

I thought for a moment and then turned back to my sister. "Allie," I told her, "I need you to do something for me."

"What's that?" she asked.

"I need you to pull your shirt up over your nose and keep it there, just like this," I said. Then I showed her what to do by pulling my own shirt up over my nose. "It'll be better to help you breathe, because of all the smoke. Can you do that for me?"

"But then I can't hold Bear," she said. And she was right. If Allie held on to me with one hand and she held her shirt with the other, there was no way she could carry Bear too.

"Allie," I said, kneeling down to look at her, "we've got to leave Bear here. We'll come back and get him later, OK?"

"But what if Bear gets scared?" she whined. "What if he gets stolen?"

"That won't happen," I told her. "Bears are a lot tougher than people. I think Bear would want you to get outside and be safe and not worry about him so much. We'll just leave him right here and. . . ." I looked around quickly and found a morning

newspaper. "I'll give him the paper to read until we get back."

Somehow that crazy idea seemed to work. Allie left Bear on the 52nd floor, sitting happily on top of *The New York Times*.

We both pulled our shirts up to block the smoke, then I took Allie's free hand and headed back into the stairwell. We were immediately drawn into the flow of people heading down. I was so afraid that I'd lose Allie again that I held on to her hand a little too tightly. She cried out in pain and I let up my grip a little.

To my surprise, Dad was almost exactly where I'd left him. I half expected him to have taken off. But he had stayed there, waiting for us, despite the smoke and the crowds. He had a wet handkerchief in front of his face and was breathing hard.

"Are you all right, honey?" he asked my sister.

Allie nodded and I explained. "I found her three floors up," I said.

"There was this man . . ." Allie said. "He scared me."

My dad just shook his head, picked Allie up and hugged her tightly.

"Listen, Allie, you have to stay close to us all the time, whatever happens," he said to her.

"We need to get out of here," I said. "A plane flew into the other tower."

Dad nodded. "I know, people are talking."

My dad had learned a lot while he was waiting for us. Some of the people going down the stairs had little PDAs called BlackBerries. They could still get the news from outside. They knew that two airplanes had hit us, and that both towers were in flames. They knew that the airplane fuel had turned our tower into a torch. And they knew we were in terrible danger.

"Coming down!" we heard from over our heads. "Coming down!"

Two men were pushing their way down the stairs, carrying a woman between them. She must have been up at the top floors when the first plane hit. The woman had burns all over her back. Her skin had turned black and was almost falling off her.

"What is it?" Allie asked.

"Nothing," I lied, pulling her tight against me. I didn't want her to see what I had seen. There's no way a seven-year-old should have to see something like that.

"Let go of me, Curtis," Allie yelled.

"In a second," I said.

The men took the burn victim past us and down the staircase, towards help. Someplace down the stairs there had to be help, I told myself. And somehow we had to get there.

But it was taking us far too long to get down the stairs. There were so many people packed into the stairway that it sometimes felt as though we were not moving at all. It really helped that people weren't pushing and trying to force the line to go faster. But still we weren't moving very fast.

Our worst problem was the smoke, which kept getting thicker. I kept a close eye on Allie to make sure that she was keeping her shirt up over her face like I told her. Every time I looked over at her, she would pull it up quickly. She'd try to make it look like she was keeping the shirt up all the time. If she started breathing in this smoke, her lungs would be in real trouble.

But in all my worrying about Allie, I'd forgotten about Dad. The smoke was hurting him a lot more than it was hurting the kid. I didn't notice until it was almost too late.

"I . . . I've got to stop and catch my breath," said Dad.

"There's no time for that," I told. "We have to keep moving."

Then I looked at him, hard, harder than I'd

looked at him ever before. He looked terrible. His face was gray and his breathing was labored. I looked around and saw a fire door; it told me that we were only on the 34th floor. I looked down at my watch and my stomach sank even further. It was 9:20 a.m. Almost a half an hour and we hadn't even gone down halfway.

I took another look at Dad and made up my mind.

"All right," I said. "We'll leave the stairwell and take a quick break so you can catch your breath. Allie should use her puffer, too. Then we have to keep moving down."

The air wasn't much better when we got off the stairs and onto an office floor. There was a lot of smoke, but it wasn't as thick.

I watched Dad as he sat on the floor and leaned up against the wall. He looked sick and exhausted. Dad coughed a weak cough, struggled for a moment and then sat up. He looked as though he was about to say something.

"You kids go ahead," he said. "I'm too old to be doing all this running down stairs. I'll be fine here until help comes."

I stared at Dad, hardly able to believe his words. How could he say something like that and expect us to just leave him up here?

"Forget it," I said to him. "Take a drink of water and let's get back on the stairs. There's no way we're leaving you here."

"That's right, Daddy," my sister piped up. "You said we have to stick together."

"I can't make it, kids. The smoke's too thick and I'm having a hard time breathing."

"Then cover your mouth," I replied, making my voice as tough as I could. My dad can be stubborn, but I can be even worse. "You're going to get up right now and you're going to continue down the stairs till we get out, do you hear me?"

Dad stared. I don't think he was expecting me to talk to him like that. To tell the truth, neither was I. I'm not the kind of guy who talks back to his parents, but now there wasn't any choice.

Dad stared a moment longer and then slowly, with much effort, he got up.

"All right," he said. "I'll try the best I can. But if I can't make it, you two go ahead. If something happens . . ."

"Nothing is going to happen until we get out of here," I said firmly. "Now cover your mouth with that handkerchief and let's go."

CHAPTER 8

Firefighters Moving Up

I should have known that my dad was in big trouble, that he was feeling even worse than he'd admit to us. Dad was an old man; he didn't have the same sort of energy that Allie and I did. I should have checked on him more to make sure he was doing all right. I should have made sure he was breathing OK and taking a few more breaks along the way. But I didn't. So when Dad collapsed on the landing between floors 18 and 19, I wasn't ready.

"Dad!" Allie and I cried out together.

He looked really bad. I had been worried when he had problems before—now he looked worse. His face was gray and his lips seemed almost blue. I had to get him somewhere he could breathe, and that meant getting down the stairs as fast as we could.

I grabbed Dad and pulled him up, slid his arm around my shoulder and grabbed him around the waist. He weighed a ton, but there was no choice left—he couldn't make it on his own.

"You're going to make it out this building if I have to carry you all the way on my back," I said to him. "If you help, it'll be easier for both of us."

Dad tried—I have to give him credit for that. He started to stumble down the stairs, putting most of his weight on me but holding himself up as best he could.

We moved a lot slower after that. People pushed past us now, and I couldn't blame them. The stairways were dark and full of smoke. Water was on the steps, dripping like a slow river. Up above us, the building was on fire. Strange sounds and cries would echo up and down the stairs. People were coughing and crying. More and more, they were desperate to get out.

"Allie, slow down," I had to keep calling.

There was only so fast I could go, carrying my dad. My little sister could move with the crowd and kept getting too far ahead of us. The last thing we needed was for her to get lost again. Around us, the smoke was getting thicker as we moved down each floor. Even worse, the line of people kept stopping. I was afraid we'd never get out like this.

When we stopped, we got news. There were guys with PDAs who logged on to the CNN site. They'd pass the news to somebody else, and soon each piece of news made it up and down the stairs. Things were bad—and they were looking worse by the minute.

I looked at my watch—9:30. We'd been on the steps for only 30 minutes, but it felt like hours. Thirty minutes and we'd only come down 40 floors. Now we were stuck in a mob of people, fighting to breathe. We were all covered in dust, dirt and sweat. I was bleeding where my arm had

scraped something. Allie was coughing and puffing her puffer. And my dad, propped up on my shoulder, looked like he was going to die. Surely it couldn't get worse than this.

Then the building began to shake.

It came less as a sound than as a shudder. There was a cloud of dust coming down the stairs, then a rush of water at our feet. The faces all around us showed our terror.

"The whole top of the tower is in flames," somebody shouted.

"What about the sprinklers?" asked somebody else.

Nobody had an answer. Even the people getting news from outside didn't know what was happening just over our heads. The top of our tower was burning, but what about all the people up there? What about the people who had gone up to the roof instead of down the stairs? And what about the rest of the building? If the fire kept moving down, we'd be burned alive here on the steps.

We were trapped. Fire over our heads, concrete walls on either side, thousands of people down below. I started to get that creepy feeling, as if I were trapped in a tunnel. I forced it out of my head. *Stay cool,* I told myself. *Save Dad, save Allie, save yourself.*

"Let's move!" somebody cried.

But we couldn't move, and when we did, it was slower than ever. There was only room for two people, side by side, in the staircase. And now firefighters were coming up one side. They were fully loaded, with all their gear and air tanks.

"Move to the right!" somebody would shout. "Firefighters coming up."

We'd all scrunch over to one side to let them pass. They were young guys, most of them, just a little older than me. I'd hold my dad against one wall as they raced up beside us. I wondered if they'd make it, if they'd get the fire out in time—or if they were doomed even then, racing up the stairs to certain death.

A couple of the firefighters stopped when they saw me holding my dad.

"You need help getting the old guy down?" they'd ask.

"No, he's my dad," I told them. "We'll make it down OK. I bet there are a lot of people upstairs who need your help."

Slowly we moved down. Fifteenth floor. Tenth floor. I think we all knew that we were fighting against time. If we could just get to the ground level, just get outside, we might be OK. If we stayed here, trapped in the stairway, we were surely going to die.

On the sixth floor, the water on the steps was almost a river. Some people in front of us took their shoes off. I figured we'd be better off with something on our feet. There was broken concrete and plaster on the stairs and in the hallways. Now we had water almost up to our ankles.

"Hang in, Dad," I told him. "We're almost out."

"C'mon you guys," Allie shouted from a couple of steps below. She was on the fifth floor landing— the big number 5 on the fire door was like a promise of life.

On the third floor, we finally got out of the stairway. We reached a large hall with escalators at one end and broken windows on every side.

Outside was smoke and dust and flashing lights. The south tower was burning like crazy with smoke pouring from all its windows. There seemed to be smoke and steam coming from all over.

Now I could hear the screaming sirens and smell the jet fuel. I wanted to run to the escalators and get out, get away, get somewhere safe. But my dad couldn't move that fast. Besides, there was a cop pointing us on. He wanted us to go down another set of stairs, further down into the basement.

That's where we headed. The three of us were together, Allie in the lead, me holding my dad. We were almost at the stairs when there was a tremendous explosion. Suddenly the walls and ceilings fell apart around us—and over us.

CHAPTER 9

Trapped

I let go of my father and jumped on top of Allie. It seemed like a huge explosion had gone off just beside us. Everything was moving—everything was falling all around us. Plaster, glass, wood, metal—it was all falling as the building shook.

In the seconds that followed, I couldn't breathe and I couldn't see. I imagined that I was already dead. There was no light, no air, no life at all. I was

not me anymore, not Curtis McIvor, but some spirit in some other world.

But if I was dead, why was there sound? Why were there sirens and creaking walls and dripping water? Why could I hear my sister crying? Her voice seemed to float out of the darkness, bringing a little light with it as I opened my eyes.

"Allie?" I whispered, my tongue sticking in my mouth.

"I can't move," my sister cried.

Neither could I. I tried moving my arms, my feet, my legs—nothing. I tried to lift my head to see, but my head bumped against something in the darkness. All I could feel was Allie beneath me, a soft warm shape that was shaking from her sobs.

"Dad?" I cried out.

I got no answer. Instead, I heard my sister crying and coughing.

"Curtis, how do we get out of here?" Allie asked.

"I don't know," I said, "but we will." The first part of that was the truth. The second part was nothing more than a hope.

We were trapped, maybe under tons of steel and

glass. We were in a little air pocket, still breathing, but who knew for how long? We couldn't move, couldn't see, couldn't even feel.

"I'm scared," Allie said. I could hear that she was trying to act brave, but how long could she keep up the act?

"Me too," I told her. "But we're going to get out. Somebody will come along and get us out of here. Or maybe . . . maybe I can dig . . ."

It was hopeless. I couldn't pull any of the rubble away, and there was no place to put it if I could. I was powerless. Trapped. No part of me could move or stretch or push.

This had been my worst fear, always my worst fear. I hated small spaces, even elevators and small rooms. I hated getting stuck in the subway or taking the train. But here I was, trapped in some tiny air space, barely able to breathe. I wanted to scream, but I didn't have the strength. I wanted to cry, but I couldn't let Allie hear me do that.

So I started to pray. *Dear God*, I whispered so Allie couldn't hear, *I don't want to die like this. I don't want my little sister or my dad to die like this. If*

You can't save me, give the kid a few more years, I prayed. *Or if we have to die, make it fast and get it over with. I can't stand this, Lord, and we all need your help.*

I don't know where those words or those thoughts came from. I don't know why I suddenly began to pray. I hadn't been to church in years, and most days I wasn't even sure there was a god up there. But now, at this last moment, the prayer just came up inside me. Even the last words came back to me, from years ago, the words of a church prayer: *In the name of the Father, the Son and the Holy Ghost.*

Then, off to one side, there was a light. I didn't know if this was the end. I thought that maybe the last part of my prayer was answered and I had just died. All I knew was that I saw light.

"Hey, we're here!" my sister cried out.

Her words brought me back to real life: we were trapped and buried—but we were alive. That was a real light out there—somebody was looking for us. Slowly the light got bigger, we heard voices and then saw moving shapes.

"Hang in, we're coming!" someone shouted.

And they did come. A firefighter with a metal bar began pulling on the pieces of building that held us. With strong hands, he grabbed the pieces of metal and plasterboard. Then, at last, the hole was big enough that he could reach through to me.

"Can you move?" he asked.

Now there was a little room for me to wiggle, not much but enough. "If you pull," I said, "and I push . . ."

He took my wrist into his hand and pulled hard. Pain shot from my arm and through my body, but there was no time to feel that. I pushed with my legs, first against nothing, then against a piece of metal. At last I pushed against something else, and the firefighter pulled me out.

I was back at the concourse level. "My sister . . . my dad," I gasped. "They're still in there."

Getting Allie out was easy once I had stopped blocking the way. As I sat at one side, the firefighter reached down. In a second Allie was out on the floor, bleeding and crying, but alive.

"Daddy!" she wailed.

"Our dad," I panted, "he's still down there. He's buried behind us, further down . . ."

I didn't have time to finish. The firefighter turned his head and pointed us towards a set of stairs on the far wall.

"I'll get him out," he said, "but you two have to move. That way—and keep going till you get out."

"But Daddy . . ." Allie cried.

"I'll get him out," the firefighter repeated. "You two get moving to somewhere safe. Fast!"

There was no more time to talk, no time to explain. I grabbed Allie and picked her up, even as she struggled in my arms. She wasn't as heavy as Dad, but she was fighting me.

"We have to go," I told her, even as we ran.

"No," Allie screamed. "Daddy!"

I tried to stay calm. I tried to stay reasonable in the most impossible moment in my life. "Allie, we have to go. The firefighter told us to go and we have to do what he says. He'll save Dad. We'd just get in his way."

Allie kept struggling, but we had no choice. I stumbled to the last stairway and past another police officer. The pain was shooting through my whole body, from my ankles right up to my skull. I must have twisted or broken something when the walls came down, but there was no time to think about that. We had to keep moving.

There were more police and firefighters as we made our way down into the basement, then up again. By then there was a whole line of police, standing side by side, telling us to keep going. Allie had stopped her struggle and now ran beside me. We were both running now, running for our lives.

CHAPTER 10

Only Rubble and Concrete

There were flashing lights all around us. It seemed as though every fire truck, cop car and ambulance in New York City was here. I looked back, trying to find the World Trade Center towers, to see if they had been able to put out the fires. But there was only one tower still standing.

I couldn't believe my eyes. Where the south tower had stood, there was only rubble and chunks of concrete. The building had collapsed. It must have fallen with a tremendous explosion, a crash that buried us, too.

Then I looked at the north tower. We had made it outside, but there were still people trapped inside. The whole top of the tower was in flames, black smoke pouring out into the air.

Allie turned to see why I was holding back. "Curtis, what are you—"

She didn't have time to finish. Before our eyes, the north tower began to fall. It began at the top, the floors that were already in flames. Then the collapse got worse, floor after floor—all falling into each other. It took only seconds, but the tallest building in New York was falling to earth.

"Oh my god," I whispered.

"Daddy!" Allie screamed.

The sound of the collapse was enormous, like a bomb had gone off. Seconds later, a tremendous cloud of smoke and dust began moving towards us. I grabbed Allie and looked for someplace that might protect us. There, just to one side, was a doorway. It wasn't much, but it was something that might save us from the cloud that was rushing at us.

"Move," I shouted, pushing Allie ahead of me.

We both crushed into the doorway as the blast of smoke and dust blew past us. I could feel the heat and the tremendous force of the blast as I huddled with Allie. It felt as though a million small stones had been thrown at my back.

Dear God, not now, not after we've lasted this long, I prayed.

But then it passed, and all that remained was smoke, dust and ashes. Maybe my ears had been hurt, but suddenly it was quiet. There was only the noise of sirens, of hissing and Allie crying beneath me.

People were wandering about. Some were confused, some injured. All of us were covered with dust and ashes. The paramedics and police officers on the scene were trying to keep things under control. But at times, they looked just as confused as we were. The scene was something out of a war movie. But this wasn't a movie—this was real.

I was beyond prayer, and my sister was beyond crying at this point. As we stumbled forward, I heard her say "Daddy" in a voice that was between a wish and a cry. There was nothing I could say to make it any better.

Behind us, in the smoking ruin, was all that remained of the World Trade Center. Once these two towers had stood tall and proud. They were symbols of our strength, our power. Now they were just a heap of rubble, so much broken glass and steel and marble. Beneath all that was our dad. Beneath all that were thousands of others, thousands of people who would never come out.

We stumbled forward. There was a little rescue

station not too far away. There seemed to be hundreds of people waiting with us for help. Some people were injured, some burned. Everyone with a serious injury was taken to a hospital, but that left the rest of us. We had scrapes and cuts and twisted ankles. We were covered in dust and ashes. The dirt was caked with our sweat and felt like a second skin. We sat, listening to news.

The news came in bits and pieces. A plane had crashed in Pennsylvania. The president was safe in Florida. The highjackers now had names. They all belonged to something called al-Qaeda. Many people were dead, or lost, or missing. They said that 50,000 people had been inside the twin towers. As many as 6,000 or 8,000 might be dead.

Our dad, I knew, was one of them.

As we sat, I kept my arm around Allie.

"Do you think Daddy...?" she asked, not quite able to finish the question.

"I don't know," I said, stepping around the truth. "Maybe the firefighters got him out, maybe he got free before the building. . . ." Then my words fell off.

What had happened to us seemed too much for words, too much to talk about in any way that made sense. The whole idea was too big to fit into words just then. Thousands of innocent people were dead because of a few madmen. But how can you talk about that in just words?

And our father was among them, buried with the police and firefighters who tried to save us. We had all tried, so hard, despite the impossible odds. Some of us, the lucky ones, had come out alive. Too many would not.

WE SPENT THE REST of the morning in a daze. Allie would cry, I would hold her, we would wait. Rescue workers came by with drinks and a little food, but neither of us could eat. Allie had used up her puffer that morning but still we had to wait in the dusty air. Finally the police gave us an OK to leave and we set out to find a phone to call Mom. We had to let her know that we were fine, that we had survived.

But even that wasn't easy. The cellphones were all giving the "no service" beep. All the pay phones we came across had huge lines of people waiting to use them. At last we gave up trying to call Mom. We decided the best thing would be to try to get home.

And that didn't work so well either.

Every subway or bus we came to was either out of service or full. It seemed hopeless. After two hours of trying to get a bus somewhere, anywhere, we were both ready to give up.

"Curtis," she said, close to tears. "I don't think we're ever going to make it home. Can we just stop walking for a bit?"

"We need to get back to Mom," I told her. "She must be worried sick about us."

"But we're all right," Allie whined. "It's Dad . . ."

"They'll find him, Allie," I said. "It's just a matter of time," I went on. It was a lie, of course. There wasn't one chance in a hundred that Dad had survived back there. Looking back, I think he was already dead when we were trapped under the rubble. But I wasn't going to tell any of this to Allie. I had to give her some hope, something to look forward to. "Look, let's get something to eat over there, and then we'll hike up to the bus station. OK?"

Allie nodded and we headed into a café on Houston Street. Now we were far enough from the twin towers site that the world didn't look like a heap of rubble and ash. This was the world we knew. It was a world of Cokes and sandwiches, counters and stools, tables and chairs. This was the real world, not the horror we had left behind.

We ate mostly in silence.

My body just ached from everything that had happened. When I sat still, the pain started all over again. The TV in the café was turned on to a local news channel and my eyes were glued to it. They kept showing pictures of the planes crashing into the buildings. Then there'd be pictures of the towers collapsing. The TV kept playing the same shots, over and over, in real time and slow motion. I made sure that Allie couldn't see the screen.

By four o'clock, it seemed as though most of the people who wanted to leave New York had already left. We were able to reach the bus terminal

at 40th Street, get cleaned up and find a bus to New Jersey. Usually, the bus goes through the Lincoln Tunnel, but that must have been closed. We took a long route up to the George Washington Bridge and over the Hudson. It took well over two hours and felt longer still. The only good thing was that I could give Mom a call on one guy's cellphone while we were travelling.

On the bus, I felt Allie fall asleep against my arm. I felt the weight of her little head, still with ashes in her hair. I thought about how much she had been through, how much she had trusted Dad and me. I thought about Dad and how he had told us to go ahead, to stay alive for him.

We had done that. We had managed to stay alive and now we had to carry on, for each other, and for our poor lost father.

CHAPTER 11

I'm Not a Hero

I don't think I've ever seen our mom as happy as she was that night. She started running towards us even before we made it off the bus. Then she hugged us for almost five minutes before we were able to pry ourselves away from her.

"I was just so worried when I saw what had happened," she said, her voice full of tears.

"Mom, it's OK, don't cry," I told her. "We're fine."

"The television kept showing all these pictures of the planes hitting the buildings. It was horrible."

"Yeah, horrible," I said. I repeated her word because I didn't have a better one. Nothing worse could ever happen in my life.

I tried to imagine what it would have been like for my mother. Stuck in New Jersey, watching all this unfold. She knew that her family was inside the north tower, but she couldn't know whether we were safe.

And for several minutes, she didn't know the worst part.

"And your father?" she finally asked.

"We don't know, Mom," I told her. "He . . . he didn't make it out with us. And we just don't know."

Then the tears really started, even mine. The three of us were bawling like crazy, standing there in the stupid parking lot. Allie and I were crying for a father we'd lost. And even my mother was crying for him, our first hint that she still cared. In truth we all cared, but it was too late to tell him.

The next day, all three of us were back in New

York. I wasn't worried about school anymore, I was worried about my dad. We had found an old picture of him, and my mom had a poster made up at a copy place. We made up two hundred posters: "Have you seen Patrick McIvor?"

Our poster was not the only one. Hundreds of families, like ours, were looking for someone they lost in the World Trade Center. On TV, we'd hear of fathers and sisters found outside the crash site. We'd hear of people who had lost their memory but were found by their families. We kept hearing stories of miracles. For a while, we were still praying for a miracle.

But my dad was dead. He was trapped in that rubble when we ran, ran to stay alive. He might have been dead when the walls came down; he might have died later. We'll never know. There are three thousand stories of terror and death locked in the remains of the World Trade Center. Those stories can never be told.

LAST WEEK, THE THREE of us went for a trip to New York City. We went to visit what is now called Ground Zero. As I stood at the fence looking in, all the pain came back. The events of the day played through my head like an old movie. I could see everything in great detail. I could play every moment, from the second we felt the plane hit the building until the time we came up from the rubble.

We had survived. So many others had not. And I think both those thoughts made me start to cry.

"Curtis, it's OK," Allie said. She had gotten strong, that kid.

"I never went to see his new condo," I said, choking on my words. "I treated him so bad."

"Yeah, but you carried him down all those stairs. You got him all the way to the third floor," Allie reminded me.

"And you kept your sister alive, Curtis," my mom added. "So look at what you did do, not at what you couldn't do."

I'm trying to do that now. At school, the kids all act as if I'm some kind of hero. But that's not true. I did what I could to keep my dad and my sister alive. I used whatever smarts I had to keep us moving, to keep us safe, to get us out.

But I wasn't a hero. The real heroes were those firefighters running up the stairs while we kept moving down. The real heroes were the cops who kept standing there, showing us the way out, while the building crumbled around them. There are real heroes buried under the World Trade Center, and we should never forget them.

I'm not a hero. I'm not one of the guys who gave up his life on September 11. But I survived to do what I did and to write our story.

Here are some other titles you might enjoy:

Show Off by PAUL KROPP

Nikki was one tough girl, or so all the kids said. She'd take on anybody, risk anything for the gang. But that was before she met Austin and began to turn her life around.

Ghost House by PAUL KROPP

Tyler and Zach don't believe in ghosts. So when a friend offers them big money to spend a night in the old Blackwood house, they jump at the chance. There's no such thing as ghosts, right?

Playing Chicken by PAUL KROPP

Josh just wanted to fit in with the guys. Maybe they did a few crazy things, but that's what fun is all about. The party rolls on . . . until Guzzo dares Josh to a race that ends in death.

Caught in the Blizzard by PAUL KROPP

Sam and Connor were enemies from the start. Sam was an Innu, close to the Arctic land that he loved. Connor was a white kid, only out for a few thrills. When a blizzard strikes, the two of them must struggle to survive in the frozen north.

About the Author

Doug Paton is a young Toronto-based writer. When he's not busy studying or travelling, he works as a magazine and newspaper journalist. Doug completed a short fantasy novel at the age of eleven, but *Terror 9/11* is his first published work of fiction.